The Menagerie Bar
(the original text)

ALSO BY MARION LONESTAR WELCH

The Wind Whisperer of Edy Swamp
Let Him Rot

The Menagerie Bar

by
Marion Lonestar Welch

Poetic Justice Books
Port St. Lucie, Florida

book design and layout: SpiNDec, Port Saint Lucie, FL
cover art: *Ava*, ©2009 watercolor by Marion Lonestar Welch

A substantially revised and modified edition of *The Menagerie Bar* was published in 2019 by La Maison.

Published by Poetic Justice Books
Port Saint Lucie, Florida
www.poeticjusticebooks.com

ISBN: 978-1-950433-57-5

Originally published 2009 by MLW

10 9 8 7 6 5 4 3 2 1

The Menagerie Bar
(the original text)

CHAPTER 1

Here I am, remembering, my mind drifting back to...

My way to The Bar to watch this crazy skinny old black guy – Chicken Charlie, that's his name. He's walking down the sidewalk, with a chicken on a leash. He has a cord of some kind tied around the neck of the red and white rooster. There's a rag with a cord wrapped around Charlie's waist; he's waving the receiver ripped off from a pay phone at the sky. Some goofy-looking couple – a man and his chicken – in the big city of Chicago.

What's he doing now? Shouting. "Hello, God, is this you? Yeah? God, I just wanna axe you a question. In fact, a friend o' mine wannas axe you a question. He wanna know if his lover is cheatin' on him."

He pushes the receiver into a hand of the unsuspecting person nearest to him.

"Here, you talk to him."

Charlie says, "Is your lover a man or a woman? You look sorta...fluffy."

The guy, embarrased, laughs back, nervous to have been picked out of the crowd by a crazy. Laughs again. Pushes coins at the old guy, throwing them on the ground, not wanting to touch the scruffy old man. The chicken knows his part, runs over; snatches the coin bites it, and takes it to Chicken Charlie's outstretched hand.

Next victim. Charlie looks her over.

"Hello there, you a fine-lookin' thing. You sure a good lookin' lady. You goin' to work this morning? You got a little extra money for a man down on his luck? Sure would be nice..." She smiles, drops a couple quarters to the chicken. Charlie smiles and waves her on.

The hustling goes on like this for some time. The rooster is getting tired; Charlie has enough money for gin now. The rooster and Charlie, just two of the more colorful residents of the three-corner transfer point of Halsted, Clyburn, and North Avenue.

Grinning, I laugh, having enjoyed the scene, cross the street, and go into the bar. I'm restless and lonesome.

Jeez, I think to myself, *I haven't even had a drink yet, and I'm listening to the conversation of a damned rooster and his master.* No wonder they call this The Menagerie Bar. Welcome.

In this Chicago bar, sex is just another substance to be used or abused, no different from the alcohol, pills or cocaine. The bar is located just off a bus transfer point near The Loop. The noise of the gin joints spills out into the three streets that came together.

The joint I drink in is dark and smoky. Mashed cigarette butts litter the floor. It smells of sour mop water, urine, ancient cigar and cigarettes. Garish, bright-colored beer and liquor signs deck the walls. No sports memorabilia, just advertisments of booze.

Working girls strategically perch their assets for maximum eye contact with any customer. Small clusters of drinkers stake out their squatters' rights on the red leatherette stools. Even though the hustlers drink and use other substances, they stay alert. Business is business.

I can drink anywhere, but this place is a good place to hide. It has a fantastic jukebox,

a lot of women, and I like looking them over. I drink while looking them over. I like the sexy feeling of alcohol taking over my body, tickling, and then pleasing my restless feeling until I'm safely numb. Saying to myself, *This drink tastes better than the last one. Think I'll have another.*

I am addicted to the music, this bar has a far-out jukebox, and the interchange of action between girl and customer is spellbinding.

The bar people are fascinating to watch. The women aren't very pretty but are available. The volume and variety of the men that come hunting females is astounding. Being a people watcher, I'm fascinated with the patrons who represent a cross section of the city – factory workers, mechanics, electricians, accountants, teachers, salesmen, ministers, hetero-, homo-, and transsexuals, as well as lesbians.

The word is out; I haven't spent any money on the whores. Gay guys will ask me am I into bondage? No. Do I like my butt spanked? No.

I am labeled a square. I am OK but square. I work a straight job – in fact, two.

I remember saying to my ex-girlfriend in Wisconsin, "I'm leaving, too. Touché, baby, I'll run off to the big city. I'm gonna find a different life."

I find it all right. It is waiting for me with a sneer on its face.

CHAPTER 2

I land in Chicago with little money, find a cheap place to live, get a job. I read the Tribune want ads; R.R. Donnelly Co. is hiring. Factory. I have no experience, but I am strong and desperate. They hire me – night shift, something to do with telephone directories. I'm going to be a jogger. Whatever the hell that is.

Meals for me are an occasional candy bar; will have to do until I get a paycheck.

I tell a fellow worker, Diane, "Everything costs so much. It's so crowded, noisy. Nobody cares about me. I can be sick in bed for a week, nobody will come to find out how I am." She says, "That's just how it is." Chicago is a big city – lots of people, too busy to care. She says, "Keep up with the speed of the conveyer, or you'll get laid off." So I jog the big packs of paper. My back is killing me; my feet hurt. Standing on concrete all night is taking its toll.

So I find this new playpen – this bar. I don't know it, but the life in this bar will leave a large impact on me. Like what these gals have suggested for a fee. Sex in any form, any flavor, any time. Wow! The availability explodes my mind. The bar hustlers boldly suggest a straight, half-and-half, blow job, trip around the world, on and on.

I don't even know what they were talking about. I really am square. My lover and I hadn't fooled around like that. Well, she and I hadn't; if she had, it wasn't with me.

I am curious about the gals at the bar, but I know a condom doesn't cover all the places on the bodies these gals use in their trade. I am afraid of disease. So I just drink, fantasize. *Oh my god, will I ever stop being excited by the bodies of women? Oh, look at that one, what well-shaped breasts, what pretty black hair.*

I smoke small Dutch Masters cigarillos, listen to the music, and watch the girls. It has been a long time between women.

The bar has a four o'clock license, so the Jewish piano plays all night. Herman, the owner, is a German Jew; that's why we call the cash register the Jewish piano. He loves to hear the tune.

Some patrons, myself included, we look the wares over. The amount of traffic is amazing. There are pickpockets, pimps, hustlers, gals, and boys – all on the meat rack, all available at any hour. Love for sale – well, not love, but sex for hire by the hour. Sometimes ten minutes will do.

It's a bizarre bunch. Some of the people seem to live here; others just float in and out while others are hawks and pick at the carrion.

CHAPTER 3

Looking across the bar – a long oval dark bar – there's a small cluster of gals partying. They're a druggie group. Money is no worry for them right now; they don't want to bother with tricks. Later when they run out of money, they are loud; every third word is *fuck* or *fucking* – a word that says nothing. "Pass the fucking salt." "How the fuck are you?" "What the fuck do you care?"

I'm off the night shift from R.R. Donnelly's; the sun is blazing bright. I'm exhausted; I stop for a drink before going home or to the next job – depending on what day it is. I signal for another beer. I don't even like beer, but as tired as I am, it seems easier to just nod my head when asked if I want a beer. It would take effort to think and order what I really want. I can still hear the people. I resent them. I drink until I can't hear them. I watch.

Bloating up on three drinks, I head for the toilet. Beer and my kidneys don't last long together; I switch what I am drinking. Walking past the dark wooden walls, my glance wavers left to the big open space at the back of the barroom. A big round old oak table stares out at me; some chairs huddle around it. They don't match – all scratched up and in different colors. The space is a dimly lit, forlorn area. Empty beer cases are stacked against the wall. A mop bucket and mop are pushed into the corner, seldom used.

Big Jackie slumps there all by herself – her body sprawled out, bleached-blond curls recklessly residing on a motionless head leaning on outstretched arms. She usually is a noisy, gregarious person, sitting up front buying everybody gay drinks, slipping stuff to special buddies.

She is a popular whore. Jackie does it all, and her price is not high. Here she is, way in the back of the barroom, all by herself like yesterday's heap of leftover mashed potatoes.

I have more urgent business than speculating on some old whore. I have to pee.

On the way back to my stool, I ask Melissa, "What's with Jackie?"

"Oh, she had a fight with her butch. A bad fight."

I nod my head.

"Hey, Melissa, give me a Cherry Heering on ice. I'm in the mood for sumpthin' different." I look up and down the bar. "Where are the working girls?" A smile, no answer. Then I realize they're in rooms in nearby trick hotels or in the backseats of cars taking care of business. "Hey, Melissa, this is good stuff. You want one?"

Melissa is the one good-looking barmaid – blond and curvy. She gives me broad smiles, sort of looks at me, and laughs. She knows I'm attracted to her, but I also know she dates the owner's butch daughter. Her business is being attractive and getting people to buy drinks.

On the way back to my barstool, I notice Jackie's butch necking up a storm with some new gal. *Jackie's butch is nuts. One swipe from Big Jackie's right paw will splat her cheating butch all over the bar wall.*

Jackie is a two-hundred-pound, *big* Polish gal – mean and deadly in a fight. She's not fat. She is fast and tough.

Crazy butch. I go far down on the right side of the bar, out of the combat arena.

Two more drinks and boredom sends me to the bathroom again. My ass is numb from sitting on this stool six hours. It is Saturday and my day off. Jackie is still there. I glare at her this time; I want her up. Something is wrong. I'm puzzled; she's positioned unnaturally, uncomfortable looking. One arm is dangling like a broken arm of a doll. I call her name. I call it again. She doesn't respond, but then she doesn't know my voice. We have never been friends. I have never liked Jackie as she is too crude – every other word is *fucking* or *motherfucker.*

Her not moving bothers me. I walk the fifteen feet over and touch her, slightly in fear that she will wake, call me a motherfucker, and smash me senseless. I give her a little nudge. I try again, no response. Her skin is cold, really cold. I put my fingers on her wrist. No pulse. *Oh...Oh, she's dead!...Oh, she's dead...just lying there, dead in a bar.*

None of her pals give a damn enough to check on her. I notice her purse and cigarettes aren't on the table. Nor is any glass. I shoot a dark look at the bar – barmaids, sloppy customers, whores and tricks, and drunks like me.

Going to the end of the bar, I yell, "Jackie's dead!" No one pays any attention. It's noisy. I yell again, this time slapping my hand on the bar. "Jackie's dead!"

"Are you nuts? Go on. Get out of here, shut up. You'll scare the customers out. You're drunk."

I'm drunk all right, but she's dead.

"Go over and touch her. She hasn't got a pulse."

I made such a fuss they call the cops. These cops are not the regulars who come in here Tuesdays for their payoff money. These cops have to work and clean up the mess.

Questions are asked, not answered; instead they are evaded. No one knows anything.

Jackie is carted out on a stretcher, looking like a side of beef – bloated, ready for butchering. The cops comment, "Another old broad OD'D." The bar patrons avert their eyes, back away as though death is like catching measles or something. The sheet falls off her face; her eyes stare, reflecting nothing, like her life. Nothing – I sense from the staring, vacant eyes. It seems to me as though she is not able to bear to see any more pain in this mean life. I cry. I have never been a friend of hers, but the shameful waste of a human's life is too painful for me.

After the grilling I get from the cops, I learn, the next time I find a corpse, leave the carrion to the crows.

Big Jackie is a sad example of floating in and out. The story is, she was married once; the guy beat the hell out of her, drank up his paycheck, fucked her silly, and left her with three kids. He split. She was frantic to take care of the kids. She heads for the bar, goes to bed with a few guys for money, and soon goes full-time into the business of sex. She drinks to get numb, uses drugs to rise above the shame and pain, goes to bed with lesbian butches as she's plenty tired of fucking men. Her life becomes the bar. She lives off it, and it lives off of her. She gets knocked up with a couple more kids from tricks.

The sad event of Big Jackie stays with me. I hate recalling the whole scene. I don't go back to the bar for weeks.

I go home. I want no more alcohol, no more life's decay. Stop the world. I want off.

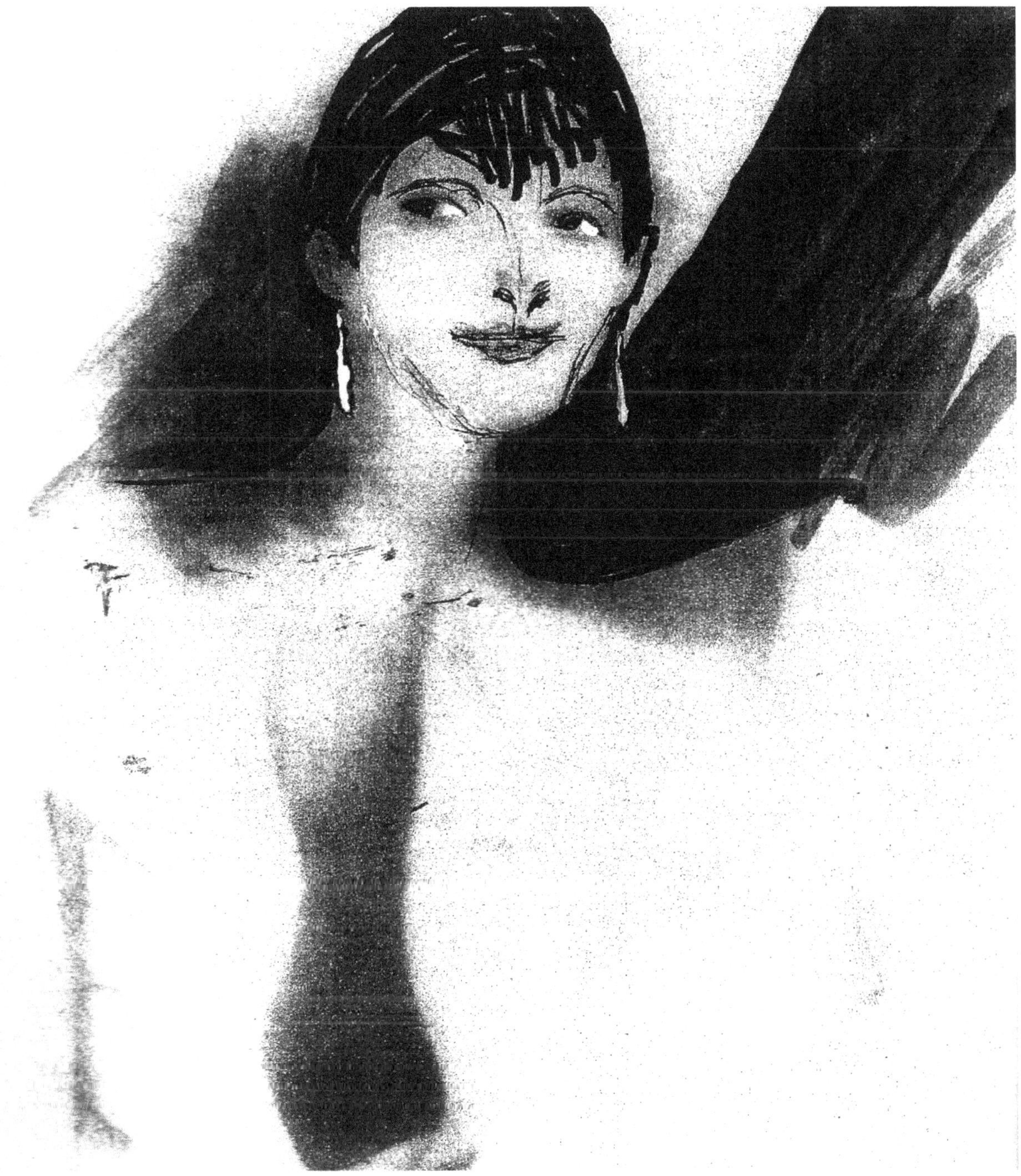

CHAPTER 4

Weeks later, returning to the bar, its darkness and noise is comforting in a sad way. It is addictive. It is a fascinating zoo of people's shame and agony. Who is here? What will happen? It is a Fellini movie in the flesh, filled with carnival-like characters.

Having a scotch or gin, listening to the jukebox – Dinah Washington's "What a Difference a Day Makes," Sammy Davis Jr. singing "Hey There," Buck Clayton's fine trumpet, lyrical and with a biting edge – tootlin' with Frankie Laine singing "My Old Flame." Great music by Eddie Condon and his group, burning up all my resistance with "When My Sugar Walks Down the Street" always brings joy to my heart. Carmen McRae's special sound "I'm Thru with Love" and her cool, cutting "Guess Who I Saw Today." "Just One of Those Things" – perfect tonal pitch, smoky, sneaky, special way of saying the feeling. Carmen McRae. What a musician, what a woman.

To hell with loneliness, and I am lonely. This great supply of music is my opiate. Sing to me baby, baby, baby all night long. The sexy message has intoxicated me.

After working the night shift at R.R. Donnelly, on top of working at the J.C. Penney credit department during the day, I'm hungry, and I stop off for a treat – a steak and baked potato for $3.77 (no tip required). I catch an all-night movie with a decent story, *Suddenly Last Summer* by Tennessee Williams with Elizabeth Taylor, Katharine Hepburn, and Montgomery Clift. Helluva story.

I am slowly wandering my way to my rooms on West Division Street. I am in no hurry to get there. My apartment is on the third-floor walk-up, flat roof. The heat sits heavy on the roof, relentless. It's too uncomfortable to sleep nights, and it's only bearable walking around half naked in the apartment days. It's the kind of hot that hurts my skin.

Months, maybe a year has gone by since leaving Wisconsin; I'm settling in to city life. Earning enough money at last, rent is paid; clothes are bought occasionally, and I'm able to eat steady.

Some of the guys on the line at work laughingly tell me they use sex toys on their girlfriends and wives with wild success. They don't hold back in their talk; they don't care I'm a female. They don't care that most on the line are female. They just talk their talk. After a few tries at getting in my pants, they disregard my gender and talk their bullshit, and I fall into the category of one of the guys. Sometimes they talk sports, food if they're hungry, but the favorite topic is sex, definitely sex.

From the way these guys talk, women seem to be panting for sex – burning up, asking a guy to whip out his dick, slap her in the face with it. And they say "eat it, take it all the way down, baby." Yep, sex is the favorite subject.

Maybe there are times a woman doesn't want to be treated gently in the bedroom. They show me catalogs with things named the pink vibrator – with a five-inch insert with a pussy tickler, guaranteed to please your partner, G-spot vibrator. Give 'em what they want, drive 'em wild. Even a waterproof gyrating penis, fun in the tub or pool.

Ye gods, all stuff I don't know about. What is wrong with my sex education? I'm curious. I'm liberal, but this toy stuff seems weird.

More dreary months go by; it's a Saturday night. I decide to skip the bar and have a quiet time at home. Read, draw, and eat potato chips.

I look out my third-floor apartment window at the building across the alley, directly into my neighbor's bedroom. *Well, there goes that idea of a quiet weekend!* There is a threesome – two guys and a girl. She's jiggling, tits flying high; she's riding on a guy's dick. He's on his back; he's jamming her, and the other guy is using her mouth. Oh my god, this sight is obscene, but it makes me hot.

I am sleeping, but it's a fitful sleep.

I want a woman – just her, just me – none of this sick stuff.

Maybe next time I'm in the bar I'll hire one, maybe Mitzi.

Mitzi has short red curly hair, a quick smile, and is shapely. She's from Milwaukee, only comes down once in a while to Chicago. She's a surprise and can play the drums. She jumps up on stage and sits in. Fun person.

Mitzi wears short skirts; when she sits on a barstool, I can see her smooth, strong tan leg and up. I'm curious about her "up." She is female with a smoking body. In my mind, I light a cigarillo, blowing thick smoke rings, imagining them touching her nipples and lingering. All I can think about now is sex. Medium-sized tits with responsive nipples that pop out hard when touched. In my mind, I collapse with delight. When I wake up, that thought of sex is still with me.

The next morning, I sleepily clump down the wooden stairs of my apartment building, cross the street to the corner grocery to get orange juice for me, milk for my cat. The oppressive heat wave has beaten my energy down; I'm dragging. My sex insanity has slowed down, too. Like the song goes, "It's too darn hot. I'd like to be with my baby, but it's too darn hot!"

A new day has begun. The neighborhood is Polish and Jewish with many small stores with shopkeepers out sweeping and mopping the sidewalks.

CHAPTER 5

Three years go by; one morning, the whole neighborhood is transformed.

Now a new wave of immigrants – Puerto Rican – has swept in overnight; they're noisy, dirty, throwing their trash on the sidewalks. The stores have been taken over by new owners, with bright-colored signs almost covering stores' entire windows. The *entire* window – ridiculous, rather than inviting – it seems forbidding, at least to me a gringo. See, I am already learning *their* lingo.

Suddenly there is a flooding of Puerto Ricans everywhere in the neighborhood. They are noisy. Sleep in shifts in their apartments occupied by several families, all in one apartment.

The men are fresh with their mouths; every female is fair game. It doesn't matter to them that they are married, and the female is married to someone else. Even little boys, barely in school, spout out, "Hey, wanna a *puta*? Wanna fuck?" They peddle their sisters. I think to myself, *Yes, but not your sisters*.

I am in no hurry to go home. The little boys are always trying to sell their sisters' asses. The mothers are screaming at the girls for being whores; the fathers are off chasing other whores. There must be some Puerto Rican couples that are happy, faithful, raising families in a good way.

I live alone; my neighbors can't believe anyone lives alone. They think it is queer that anyone lives alone in a *huge* five-room apartment. They think I am queer. It is a title of comparison I accept with pride.

Friday and Saturday nights are hideous with the din of fighting, blaring music coming out the apartments, smashing of broken bottles, screams of the wives and girlfriends beaten up by the drunken men in their lives. The wail of the sirens from the cops' cars, the loud stomping of the cops up the stairs, the nightsticks pounding on the doors, the screams, the swearing – the insanity of it all.

For some strange reason, the little Puerto Rican kids pound on my door to give 'em refuge. They know I live alone and have room. I let 'em in; I put them on the couch, my upholstered chair, my bed. My bed! It's a full house this Saturday. I don't know why, but I feel sorry for them.

Bootsie, the black cat with four white boots, and I go out on the small back porch. I have a cigarette, blowing the smoke out into the air. From the porch, I look out and down on the alley. What little air there is comes dragging in on its feet in exhaustion. It's hot in Chicago in the summer. Sweltering, smothering hot. I wonder if my neighbors feel as lost as I do.

In the very early morning, neighboring apartments are finally quiet, so my little houseguests creep home, waving 'bye, and grinning. Such sweet little kids to come from such chaos. Of course, they have eaten every cookie, cracker, and drank all the pop and fruit juices I had. I was lucky to grab one Pepsi for myself.

CHAPTER 6

After the awful weekend scene, I goof off, stop at the bar. Even its action seems calmer than the Division Street din. If it is too early for me to drink the hard stuff, I order a coke, listen to music until my eyes start to close, then head home. Home is the studio and living quarters third-floor walk-up on West Division Street. Rent is cheap. I can have my art studio. I am still trying. Transportation is good. Neighborhood is exhausted and exhausting. It is definitely a low-rent district, but it is what I can afford – $125 a month, five rooms. It is a good deal for me. If only the people around here were different, it could be nice.

Still staying with my bad habit, I indulge.

After work, I stop off at the bar. I go over to the jukebox, play a Sam Cooke number "You Send Me." Sam's great voice sure does send me. Makes me think of the most beautiful girl I have yet to meet. I am an incurable romantic.

I am tired. I drag myself up on a barstool, order a Coke, close my eyes. Sammy Davis is singing "What Kind of Fool Am I?" *Do I have to ask*? I order another drink. Then Roy

Orbison comes out with "Pretty Woman." The lyrics all talk to me.

Oh yeah, I remember a pretty woman or two.

Upon opening my eyes again, I survey the bar – a long oval-shaped bar, dark wood. Busy. Worked by two barmaids, not particularly attractive, but they know how to bullshit and serve drinks. I'm sitting there surrounded by all this smoke, noise, studying the people. It is amazing to me how people speak words but do not say anything. Nor do they wait to hear the answer to an inane question. During my musing, I run a fast check on who is sitting at the bar or leaning against the wall. Have to keep all the players in mind. It is a rough bar; now and then, all hell breaks out. Barstools, shot glasses fly everywhere. If I am not careful, I can be in range of danger.

There is one gal, Gerry, who has lost her right eye getting hit by a shot glass from a fighter's toss. The shot glass went sizzling across the bar, struck her in the head. She lost her eye. She has been given free drinks for life in exchange for not suing Herman and the bar. She gladly took the deal. For an alcoholic, free drinks for life is heaven. She thought it wonderful and promptly proceeded to become a happy, sloppy drunk. Sometimes not so happy and sometimes when she is, she gets a crying jag and goes into the toilet, closes the door, and passes out. We all want to kill Gerry then especially when we need to pee.

Not all action takes place nights; usually in the day, the bar scene is calmer. A few johns in business suits will stroll in for a *matinee* before taking the train home to the wife and kids. What hypocrites, as long as these guys get their rocks off, they don't think about disease or leaving a load of cum garbage in a whore's belly. Sometimes they plant a trick baby.

I can NOT believe these hustling mothers bring their kids down to this dive, daytime to show off the kids to their other whoring friends. I watch it. But this bar *is* their life. Unbelievable. I thought my early life was horrible but not like this. My big brother had sexually molested me plenty. I remember.

CHAPTER 7

Seasons change, drinkers don't. Sitting and sipping, pondering "where is love? Am I crazy?" I order another drink, glare at the content, feeling gloomy. I want someone to love me, a woman. I can wait; I'll find the right one. To hell with sex. I'll probably never find a girl. I'm shy. Why is everything so complicated? I go into a gloom of depression. I can still hear the people. I think they can read my thoughts and are laughing at me. I feel miserable.

I am sitting at the bar, sipping a scotch, philosophizing about the sadness of the human race and me being in my running shoes for the race. This well-dressed platinum blond comes in, looks around, and sits down two stools from me. She definitely gets my attention. She has an amazingly beautiful face, fine nose, an assured posture. A helluva figure. The artist in me is alerted, so is my libido.

She is dressed in beige slack suit with champagne shell. Her shell is the kind that makes me want to see through the cutout pattern on the top of her blouse. What is under it? I've been at the bar too long. On earth too long. My mind is unihibited, and I want to see the slope of her breasts, the light pink of her nipples. I am positive that they will be pink and have pert faces. She is classy, definitely classy.

I have never seen her at this bar. I am curious. What is she doing in this cesspool of the city? Slumming? For what? Boys, girls, dope?

The mystery is soon answered. Some of the working girls come in; they know her. "Hi, Ava." She smiles a quiet, contained Mona Lisa smile. I think she must be in the "life." There she is, looking regal for a lady in a rotten racket. She declines drinks from several guys, smiles, shakes her head no. She is different. Turns back and talks to girlfriends.

I look at this pretty young woman again. I feel depressed. I order another gin. Shit. I don't want her to be a prostitute. In my mind, I cannot call her a whore; it seems crude. Reading the "tea leaves" in the bottom of another gin, I mull it over, but no matter the terms, the glaring image of her being with some guy makes me furious, of her being with anyone other than me eats me up with jealousy. In my mind, I am already with her – intimately, mutually delicious. What the hell is the matter with me? Insanity overtakes me. I have passion for this woman. I have had too much to drink; I have sat looking at all the sex transactions going on for months. I am overdue.

This woman excites me.

I order another gin, greedily guzzle it. I look at her. She smiles. Oh my god, she smiles. What a beautiful smile, small dazzling white teeth. Her blond hair is short, showing off her gentle jawline. She is pretty. She looks away. Oh my god, she looks away! Who is she looking at? My heartbeat speeds up. What the hell is the matter with me? The muscles of my stomach are tight; I am alert. I have to get out of there.

Outside, the cool air clears my head somewhat, but that damned beautiful woman makes me feel like she has yanked a piece of skin off my body. Like I am a grape, and she just peeled me. I feel like I have a sore, a gaping hole in my body.

But I want to see her face again. That perfect Rossana Podestà face, that Brigitte Bardot face again.

I go back to the bar the next night and the next. She isn't there. I feel depressed. Shit!

CHAPTER 8

Weeks go by.

I go circling back to the bar night after night looking for her, but she doesn't show.

She is in that *other* world – her world. The one that I don't know where it is or what it is.

Work, drunken weekends, cab rides home alone. I go to the Chicago Art Institute, attend concerts at Orchestra Hall, watch imported movies, and try different restaurants for different ethnic food. Still check the bar every now and then, hoping to see that beautiful woman Ava. Mine is a stupid, hollow life.

While sitting around at the bar waiting for the bookie Tommie to drop off my winnings, I amuse myself talking and listening to other bar people. A kid, a young girl in her teens really, comes up to me. She tells me her story. I am known to have empathy; I'm a natural sucker. She lays it on. I listen.

She has hustled, freelance, no pimp, a few months; she hates hustling, and it scares her.

She doesn't want to end up like Vickie, the cute colored girl. That pretend neo-Nazi son of a bitch all dressed up in an SS uniform. He took Vickie to the corner trick hotel, bound her up, beat her to death with wire coat hangers. Cries for help were drowned by the Saturday night roar.

Slicing her body into red rents. Disproving his superiority as Vickie's red *blood proves* we *are all the same*. Then this sick, sissy bastard tosses her out the window down into the alley to splat like some pathetic package of garbage.

The little gamin tells me the sad story and doesn't want to die like Vickie. Nope.

The kid is trying to come off the street.

Doesn't she know there are tremendous obstacles to overcome? The prospective landlord is afraid. They're afraid she'll bring tricks into their house. Plus she looks like a real kid, probably lying about her age. And the street person has to be leery too of the prospective landlord, probably a sneaky old pervert looking for a freebie.

Life is a land mine.

Can the street person wanting to change last long enough to get out from under the grinder?

She is desperate.

She tells me she knows what she has to do; she is aiming on getting out. She has to or go nuts. She refuses to accept this type of sadistic survival. She will rather die than live in this shit pile. She is a fast-running alley cat who has to land on her feet.

I give her fifty bucks. What the hell? Fifty bucks is my track winnings from yesterday. What the shit. I don't do this often, in fact, never before. I tell her to go get on a Greyhound, go far as she can. Go. I don't know if she makes it. It's like a 70 to 1 odds. No one sees her around anymore.

CHAPTER 9

I'm getting to be a regular.

Staring into the bottom of my glass of Johnny Walker, amber in color, feeling mellow, just killing time.

Listening to Tony Bennett singing "The Shadow of Your Smile," I start to think of that good-looking woman Ava. She had rather a Mona Lisa smile. She is still on my mind, or whatever part of my anatomy remembers her. No luck. She isn't at the bar. I drink more booze, listen to more music.

I stop off at the bar after work. I have given up on ever seeing her again. Then…she comes walking in, looking like a luminous, serene angel. *I should have remembered* there are angels of light and angels of darkness.

She looks around, sees me, smiles. Oh my god, she *is* beautiful. I smile back. She walks farther down the bar to where some girls sit. They all laugh. What are they laughing about?

At? All my emotion and desire must be hanging on my face. I am so easy to read. I'm uncomfortable. I'm still a hick.

They look my way, laugh some more. She looks my way again, slowly turns on her stool, gets off, and comes toward me. It is a mesmerizing walk. She smiles a slow, deliberate, sweet, challenging kind of smile, locks eyes with me, and asks if I will buy her a drink. I signal the barmaid; I order two drinks. I don't know what she drinks, but *the* barmaid does. Ava sits on the stool; we talk small talk. She has been shopping downtown on Michigan Avenue. She turns; her knees touch mine. I hold my breath; the touch is electric. Ava is electric.

An hour later, I am helping her with her packages, and we are going out the door.

I hail a cab. My body is racing; inside I am shouting. I am with her. She is beautiful. Hurrah, hurrah. I feel like I have just made a touchdown, hit a home run.

I am drunk with her nearness, her perfume. It is light but seductive. I put my arm around her waist; I draw her close to me. The cabbie is peeking in the rearview mirror. Kissing her on the cheek, I pull her even closer. God, how I want this woman. She gently pushes me back, puts her finger on my lips, smiles, says, "Wait."

My mind says, *Wait! Wait, shit*. I do wait.

CHAPTER 10

We finally get to her buiding in an expensive area, Marine Drive. I am excited, in agony.

We go upstairs to her second-floor apartment. The couch and chair are purple velvet. there are a couple of well-framed paintings by Portales. There are sterling silver cigarette urns and lighters. It is nice. Her place is relaxing, in contrast to my worn-out, secondhand, mismatched furnishings. She takes the packages, puts them on the couch. She goes into another room; she kicks her shoes off and comes back still wearing her black fur hat. I want to rip her clothes off, but I don't have to, Ava takes her blouse off, hands it to me, smiles. I smile back. Her black bra hides her fine shaped teats. Her skin is light cream. My eyes run down her stomach to a red thong. I kiss her stomach, and I take the thong off. Her triangle of hair is dark brown, but the hair on her head is blond. How could that be? Women.

I kiss her clitoris. It is soft and sweet. She presses my head back for more. I am willing. She is hot looking; I am just hot. We barely take time to breathe.

I wake up in the morning in her bed. The covers are white, with massive pillows, mountains of pillows everywhere. The mattress is firm, comfortable; it is a king-size bed. No wonder I have no trouble when I go down on her to nuzzle her female nectar. Damn, she tastes good, this most delicious woman.

The night table on my side has a fancy lamp with prisms of crystals. I can smell fragrances from her many perfume bottles on the light-colored mahogany dresser. I smell the fragrance on her near me. I glance at her, sleeping soft and sweet. It is wonderful, relaxing in a special way, gazing at this mysterious, generous woman; I want her again. Oh my god, how I want her again.

Ava's name is written in my head. No other female will do. To be that way is to be in agony. Haunted, listening for her voice, and watching for the face that matches that special name.

I turn slightly, trying not to disturb her. I glance out the eyelet curtain covering the window. Maybe Ava will wake up soon, maybe. It is snowing huge lacey flakes, matching the pattern of the curtain; the flakes fall like fluffy feathers. It is beautiful, peaceful.

I flip the sheet off her upper body. Beautiful nipples, I put my mouth completely on one; it comes to attention.

She wakes up, puts her hand out, musses my hair, smiles, and pushes my head sideways on her breast. Kissing her, I move behind her, we spoon, I hug her. I fondle her breasts. I love the feel of her. I feel the heat of our bodies, and she is the most no-holds-barred, generous female I have ever been with in my life. Ava teaches me sexual moves I don't even know. She is killing me with pleasure.

Pleasures more than the flesh although I grin at the changes she has made in me. I'm happy, confident, and loose. Quick to love, I love everything – kids, cats, and dogs. Everything is wonderful.

Going back to touching Ava, I feel excited, delighted to see the grace of skin lead to the slope of her breast. It makes me breathe quick; as if to make a noise, the move would frighten off the magic of the beauty of a butterfly, if one was perched on her.

I love the smell of this new woman, the light, alluring fragrance of lilac, so feminine, and then so heady. I want my head back in her secret black forest. I want to make love to her, please her.

I kiss her on her soft, satiny stomach. The perfume mingles with the glow of lovemaking. It is heady. I ask her for the perfume's name. She says, "*Je Reviens*."

"What does that mean?"

"I shall return," she says.

"Oh my god. Yes, always."

We spent the weekend together. It is exciting and wonderful. There is no discussion of money (hers or mine), what we do for our separate living, politics, or religion.

We lie in bed sharing English muffins smeared with imported strawberry preserves; we share strawberry-flavored kisses too. She has a great mouth, like little fishes nibbling then turning barracuda. I nuzzle her throat; she laughs, dropping some strawberry on my chest. She bends down, kissing my chest quickly, going to my nipple. Her mouth stays there. I am startled, alarmed; I didn't know what to expect as I had never been touched like that before. It is wonderful. My mind flows into her. It is a different feeling; I feel chills in my lower legs. This woman has just taken any hold out of innocence from me. She can touch me anywhere she wants, anytime she wants, and I love it.

I am so elated and emotionally drained that I do not object when she tells me she cannot see me again for a week as she is flying to Jamaica, but she will call me. We have not exchanged phone numbers; we do now. We exchange many more kisses. I cannot touch her often enough. My eyes love to look at her.

A week seems a long time – to me anyhow – but I have to get it together and go to work. What a different world.

She walks me to the door, turns her face up to me to be kissed; I kiss her mouth, lingering. She holds my hand, asks me my name. I laugh. She kisses me on the cheek. She doesn't know my name. *It blows my mind, with all the physical sex we have done this weekend, to not know my name is ridiculous. I know hers.* We exchange telephone numbers; apparently we are going to get together again. *She doesn't know my name?* It is Chris, your lover.

Physically, I am delighted, tired, but mentally wondering. *Who is this woman I love? What kind of life does she live?*

How many telephone numbers *does* she have? How does she know who she is talking to? I walked away dazed but physically delighted. Crazy world.

My name is Chris. Chris and I will be back, Ava. I turn, wave, and smile. I smile all over. Crazy world. Inside my body, I'm singing, "On a clear day, you can see forever."

I ride down in the elevator to the lobby, thinking about my weekend with Ava. I smile to myself. "Goodbye for now, Ava in wonderland. I have an important date – work. But I shall return to you." Songs of Edith Piaf are singing in my mind. I am happy.

CHAPTER 11

Walking into the night shift, the guys looked at me and roar. Timber! She got laid. Look at her! Come on, tell us! I couldn't; I just nodded and grinned. What goes on between a woman and me is private. Oh my god, the memory is great. My mind is captured; now I want to live and make love to Ava forever.

I am in a dangerous place and don't care one damn bit. I'm in love, neither knowing nor caring I leapt in with both feet. Later, much later, thinking back on this whole Ava-Chris thing, if I had been wise, I would have run away, had a one-night stand. It was too hot, too fast to last. Instead, I ran to her; her beautiful face, her dazzling smile, her fragrance encircled me like a velvet octopus. I am doomed, drowning in her delightful body. I could not get enough. *Je Reviens*. I shall return, many, many times.

We go along throughout the summer, calling each other, and meeting at her place when she invites me. The sex is always the same – screamingly good. There are many things we did not discuss. I know very little of a personal nature about her. Like, has she been married? Are her parents still alive? Where do they live? Where did she grow up? Where did she really work? I knew it wasn't on the street or at the bar. I was pretty sure she didn't have a pimp. I never saw one on the scene. Ava's mode of operation is a mystery. For some reason, some insane reason, the mystery didn't bother me. It was okay with me. I didn't want to deal with the problems; I only wanted her in my arms.

She has little curiosity about me. She is mainly in the now, and the past didn't seem to count. She called me two or three times one afternoon; I wasn't home. When I saw her again, she mentioned my not being home when she called. It apparently annoyed her; she wants to know where I have been. Her voice is tinged with terseness – and possessiveness. I am surprised. I answer her that I had gone to the Chicago Art Institute. She looks at me quizzically as though she does not believe me. Why would she not believe me? Ava, Ava, I love you.

I have mentioned to her that I am an artist. True, I have never shown her anything, but she has never shown any interest, and I sure as hell am not going to invite her to my run-down building where my apartment and studio is – and not to my wild neighborhood with all those horny guys and the little kids yelling *puta* (whore). This could get complicated. *Puta* – maybe she understands Spanish. I don't want her insulted. Better not bring her here. If these guys saw a woman this good-looking, they would burst into a riot.

Another year passes.

I am reading a book *Lust for Life* while riding on the Division bus going east to the transfer point to Ava's place. She lives in the expensive part of town on Marine Drive. I phone her, asking if she needs anything. "Yes, a quart of hand-squeezed orange juice, quart of 2% milk, two packs of Alpine cigarettes, and your hot body." This pleases me. That statement says she needs to have me next to her. I'm not alone in this addiction. We are a couple.

Why am I so in love with her? She doesn't draw a bath for me nor cook a meal for me. We don't like the same movies; in fact we never go to the movies or to concerts or anywhere outside of her apartment. Well, yes, we do go grocery shopping. I do cook an occasional meal; my aunts have trained me well. I cook plain Midwestern food – roast chicken, pot roast, St. Louis ribs, and sauerkraut. I seldom cook, but it is gobbled up like it was gourmet. Very flattering. My home-cooked food brought out a tender side of Ava. After our stomachs were full, we would take naps, cuddling. She was a grateful child, purring away. When she thought it was her turn to provide food, she orders delivery.

We do go downtown to shop at Marshall Fields for clothes, perfume for her. She surprises the hell out of me, buys me gray silk pajamas one time. Impromptu. Isn't my birthday, Christmas, or any special occasion. I wear them when we watch TV.

We went along this way for months, then over a year.

CHAPTER 12

I bring her a white-flocked Christmas tree – six feet tall, full of magic, certainly full of love. I have been alone in my apartment, feeling a great empty space in me where I need Ava. I am overcome with the need to show her how much I care, how special she is to me. We always have extraordinary sex, but I want her to know she is my darling, not just an object. It is Christmas, and I love Ava, and I feel she is my family.

Phoning her, "Hi, it's me, Chris. You all right? I was watching the snow coming down. It looks so pretty. Like you. I just want to hear your voice. Am I drunk? No. Do I want to come over? Yeah. I want to come see you. I'm bringing you something. Uh-huh – a surprise. No, I won't tell you. It's a surprise."

I took a cab to her apartment, with the huge tree stuffed in the cab. I had to sit in the front passenger seat. The huge tree took up all of the back seat. I paid the guy; he looked at me like I was crazy. Then the tree and I staggered, bumping the tree into the elevator. Thump, thump, bump to her door. Pound, pound. "Open up!"

At first she is sort of annoyed. Where will she put it? She runs all over the living room in a distracted way. "Maybe here. Oh, no. It's so big. Why in hell did you bring this big thing?" She stands up on her toes. "Oh, it's beautiful." And she bursts out crying.

I am confused. Ava's crying for christ's sake. I am trying to please her. Not ready for her tears; neither is she. She has no Kleenex near. I go to the bathroom and get a couple and hand them to her.

She sinks onto the velvet couch, loudly blows her nose, and explains she has never received anything so beautiful and unexpected as this white-flocked Christmas tree.

"I love it. I just adore it. Beautiful, just beautiful. Oh, Chris, I love you."

Her face got scrunched up, and she cried and cried. My emotions were mixed; I put my arms around her, and we walked to the bedroom. I just held her, patted her hair, kissed her cheek. No sex.

Then Ava gives me a gift of trust.

In a very small voice – childlike, in contrast to her well-rounded adult female body – she began to tell me the secret of her childhood life. Her mother and she never had a Christmas tree. They put up Christmas cards, candles, and candy. They were extremely poor, living in rooming houses and flop hotels on Madison Street in the west side of Chicago. It was just the two of them; they stayed away from other people. The mother went to work so they could eat and pay the rent. Ava's part was to be quiet, not run in the halls nor let anyone in the room, not answer the door if anyone knocked. Hers was mainly a world of no – no playmates, no school. She was nonexistent.

Her mother worked nights as a dice girl, and being a pretty young Irish Appalachian with fine features attracted men. They came to the bar to drink and see the pretty dice girl. Some tried to date her; they didn't get very far. She went straight home to her platinum-haired baby. She stopped at a diner and bought Ava hot dogs, doughnuts, and candy. The two of them went on this way, surviving for years. Ava's mother was afraid of men; something bad had happened down in West Virginia, and she ran. She got on a bus and ran.

Finally, one night, a different kind of man came up to her little dice table, smiled at her. He had a strong face, eyes appreciative of her good looks but not hungry to eat her. His name was Tom. Tom Skokonavics. He was a house painter. Polish, handsome, black-haired with amazing blue eyes. He had no family here; what was left was in the old country. He smiled a warm smile. She smiled back.

The dice girl began to look forward to his coming to the bar and visiting with her. One night they went out for a sandwich. He lived in a room also, in a different cheap hotel. They went to his room. They kissed a long, claiming kiss. They had fierce sex. They were in love. They made plans to get a small apartment and be together.

And so it came to be that the man and the woman – fiercely, passionately, insanely dependent on one another – had this one small problem. Ava.

So little Ava was sent outside so they could have sex. The man craved his wife more and more and did not like some other man's kid around. The young wife sensed and feared her ardent husband would leave her if he couldn't be with her when he wanted to. Ava was her child, but this wife was obsessed with this man. She had to have him. The child became the outsider; she was the problem.

So Ava was shoved outside more and more; she blended into the shadows of the hallways, back porches, and alleys. She drifted farther and farther off. Street people began to notice her, not in a curious way, not in a protective way, but in a predatory way. For those who did not work nor have money, this child presented herself as opportunity for gain. She was easy; she was frightened and alone.

Ava soon learned these depraved old sons of bitches got turned on from her crying when despoiling her ten-year-old body. She wised up, would not give them that added pleasure, and stopped crying, then wised up again and found crying brought big tips. Ava graduated in sex cum laude.

After several years, she was totally streetwise. She went from being used as a sex toy until she had found out sex was a game. She was the commodity. Sex gave her control; men were easy. Now she had money and was independent.

She wiggled into my arms, kissed me on my cheek, said she loved the tree and me. We went to sleep.

We never discussed her childhood again.

I wake up; she is gone from our bed. I go looking for her in the apartment. I find her intently reading directions on a box of Jell-O.

"What are you doing?"

"I'm going to cook for you. I know you love Jell-O."

I am overwhelmed. I sit down at the breakfast table, drink a glass of milk, watch her, and adore her. She loves me.

I get up, walk over to her after she put the Jell-O in the fridge, kiss her, hug her, and lead her to the bedroom.

She has a most perfect shapely rounded ass with a slender kitten body. She is a delight. I love how she moves her legs when we make love, grabs my hair, pushing my head down. I love to hear her moan. We sixty-nine. She likes to be slapped on her butt; she gets excited, raises her head. I clamp her back, bringing her body down, locking on her clitoris. She screams in pleasure. She is mine.

There has never been such a woman in my life. I love her. I love sex with her.

We have been seeing each other, one or two nights a week for months, but we never move in with each other. We never talk of it either. There is a lot we do not talk of.

One weekend, I arrive at our appointed time. When I step in her living room, there was a young platinum-haired boy, about four years old, there. His name is Jason; he is her son. Her son! She has never mentioned having a son, never mentioned being married. Married? Grow up. Her life is a mystery to me, but her body is not. I still don't know how she can afford such an expensive apartment.

Now and then, Jason will be there at her home. He is a nice, shy child with green eyes like his mother. We read books I bring him, we draw pictures together, and I have brought him a huge set of oil crayons and paper. He is proud of his artwork and runs to his mother with the latest effort. Like a good mother, she will ask me to stick it on the fridge.

There never is any mention of the father. Another mystery. I ask where Jason stays when he isn't with her. She said her mother's – Jason's grandmother. That was the end of the subject. I tried to get more answers, but Ava freezes me out. (Is this the same mother that put her out on the street when she was such a young kid?) It's all a mystery. When did Ava and her mother get together and make up? I never knew.

I take Jason to the zoo and the park; he loves it, is very excited, but Ava has an aversion to going out of the apartment.

CHAPTER 13

I'm still working at R.R. Donnelly and freelance painting on the side.

The guys from work invited me to a guys' night-out party – food, booze, and porno flicks. It was gonna be great, big teats, fantastic asses, every position imaginable. It was gonna be fun. Looking back on it all now, I wish I had never agreed to go to that damned party.

We were all sitting around, munching thick ham sandwiches, drinking Budweisers, vodka over ice, salted nuts; when after gabbing guy talk, one of the guys said, "Bring on the porno." We had seen a couple of asshole-drilling flicks and one with a young, pigtailed girl playing the part of a seduced babysitter doing a half-and-half. The guys were moaning in appreciation of the pussy parade.

I got up and had to go to the toilet. I came back into the room to see three hot lesbians in action. One girl was spread-eagled with a dark-haired lesbian, licking the bottom one's pussy; the bottom one liked it, wiggling in encouragement. A short-haired redhead is sitting on the bottom one's face. The guys are making hot comments; they are getting off. The gals shift positions. I think I am having a heart attack. My body jumps. It cannot be! It is impossible! My Ava is the blond on the bottom! My Ava! I thought I would puke. I will kill her, the bitch. Not only that but Mitzi is the redhead sitting on my sweetheart's face. Goddamn these bitches. Damn their whoring asses. My girl is a porno queen!

I tell the guys I'm sick, I must have eaten something bad, and I'm going home. I lurch out of their apartment, catch a bus home. I can't hold it back; I cry, right out in public. I'm a private person. I don't cry where anyone can see me. But there I am blubbering, not giving a damn. I can't wait to get to my place, to lie down somewhere to hide, to die. Oh my god, I love Ava. How could she?

We have not seen each other for a while. I cannot imagine looking at her again.

She has been busy and has not called. I am grateful.

The phone rings, and Ava's soft voice says, "Hi, lover. Come over. I've been missing you." She meets me, opens her door, kisses me passionately. I return the kiss, walk her to the bedroom. We have sex and more sex. It is grand. *How can it be? How can I touch her?* But I do.

She gets up, smiles at me, and asks if if it was good for me. I get this insane flashback view of her in the porno and say, "Yes. Was it as good as you got it in your porno with Mitzi?"

She flies out of the bedroom, down the hall, and into the kitchen. I hear some kitchen drawers opening and closing, banging, and she swoops out of the kitchen back to the bedroom, with a strange look on her face and a shiny steak knife in her hand.

She heads straight for me, "You son of a bitch. You sat there, watching, laughing at me. You dirty son of a bitch." She lunged at me, stabs me, again and again. The pain is horrible. I roll off the bed, trying to get away from her and that goddamn knife. Leaping, I jump up out of bed. *I have to get out of her apartment.* I try to find my clothes. *Forget them. I have to get out.*

I have stab wounds, blood running all over me; I am slipping on my own blood. I have been stabbed in the face, my nose, and my arms where I had tried to protect myself. She is still screaming curses, flying around, trying to kill me. We both fall down slipping in the blood. She stabs me in the stomach, my upper legs. I feel like I'm going to puke and pass out. I had been in a half sleep after sex, but I am sure awake now.

CHAPTER 14

Buck naked, I get up, heading for the door. I don't care. I am out in the hallway. Safe. Running down the hall to the elevator, I punch the button for the lobby. No one sees me.

She is insane, crazy, a madwoman. I have to get to a hospital. I think I am dying. Ava tried to kill me. Ava has stabbed me; she hates me.

I have no clothes on, tiptoe right past the sleeping desk clerk. Wow. There I am bathed in my own blood from wounds made by my sweetheart. Oh my god, how could this be? I stagger, leaving a trail of blood behind me. I lurched through the lobby undetected; bursting outside, I have made it I am burning with pain but freezing my ass from the winter snow; I am walking barefooted.

Jeez, I hurt.

Into the black early morning, bitter cold weather, weaving from pain and fear, I stagger down the sidewalk. I am confused, not knowing what to do or which way to go. I am naked, have no money, but I have a lot of bleeding wounds.

What the hell would I do if I met somebody at this ridiculous hour in this ridiculous condition? I have gone a couple of blocks when, son of a bitch, here comes a guy toward me, dressed in a long coat. My mind is so confused; I don't ask for help. I stare at him. I hold my breath. I just keep looking at his face. He stares at my nakedness in disbelief, and when we have met, I say, "Good morning." His eyes get big; he says nothing. We keep on walking in opposite directions. I keep on walking, shivering, and bleeding. No squad car passes by, just me staggering naked into the freezing early, early morning.

I look like a modern day Frankenstein. I give up. I close my eyes, sink down, sinking onto the snow-covered sidewalk like water into sand. Losing it.

I collapse. Some cop sees me crumpled on the sidewalk. From his squad car, he calls for an ambulance, which takes me to Weiss Memorial Hospital.

Next I was on a gurney, rumbling down the hospital hallway to the emergency room. An orderly in a maroon outfit is pushing me; he babbles inane shit in my ear. "Boy, you sure must have gotten caught cheating on your sweetie, and she sure made lunch out of you." I wanted to strangle him, but I was too weak, and blood was running down into my eye. Little queer prick.

CHAPTER 15

Six months has gone by.

I am in a state of repair – unreal – trying to regain my balance. I am somewhere in between loving you or being lost. I keep twirling around like a spider on the water of a large lily patch, busy going nowhere but diligently pursuing the fantasy. When I gaze off into the distance trying to gain perspective, sunlight sabotages my attempt, resulting in glimmers glancing off an unnamed image. I tread water in this sea of emotional torment; the only call that comes to mind is "I love you." Love you?

I love you still, which means my senses are in a squalid place. This picture window presents an image; it is an Ivan Albright painting. I still cringe from the impact, with the thought of his second portrait of an ulcerated Dorian Gray. It now reminds me of me – the wounds of sins, the results of the vicious violent life of the world of the bar and its people. How we devoured and retched back our individual reactions to boot grinding evil. Curses took the place of caresses.

You hate me. You slashed and stabbed me twenty-four times. It was after I told you I knew what you did for a living. I had seen a porno of you. You were the star. My reaction was violent. I thought I would puke or pass out. I was in love with you. I couldn't breathe. My body scalded in denial. And there I was at this Saturday night party, with all those guys yelling and cheering, screaming obscene things about my sweetheart. My heart died.

I remember the violence, the pain, being wheeled on the gurney to the emergency room, the swabbing of my punctured body with green soap. The nurses couldn't find which stab wound to stop first. The flood of blood was everywhere. I was nauseated, my head swimming. The bright overhead lights hurt my eyes. The sutures sting. The police asking me questions that I couldn't answer – would not answer. Ava, you led a secretive life, had a small son.

Who did this? Why? What is your relationship? I didn't want to say we were gay. And now I knew you were in a gray shadow world. No cops.

And here I am, months later, in a rented boat in Lincoln Park on the lagoon. I always head for water when I feel sad and have things to think out. Here I am wounded physically, emotionally. Mentally trying to heal, my mind says, "I love you."

Am I mad? What sickness sits on my stomach, smiling at me like a smug tiger licking its paws, playing the waiting game? I am an artist. I create. I don't destroy, but this thing between us is destructive. With your street knowledge, you sense the soft parts of me and head for them like a pit bull, with your shining stainless steel teeth, ripping them out as choice carnal offerings. And I do you no good; as the willing victim, I encourage you to hone your killer instincts. I confuse you with my spiritual belief in life, in goodness, in wanting to help each other.

Back home in my rented room, looking into a mirror, I see the ugly scar where the knife went through the wall of my nose. The scar is raised from my regular skin, like an angry red worm, irregular, twisting, showing its contempt of order. I look strangely deformed to me.

"I'll rip your face off," you said.

How could you do that to me?

"I hate you! I hate you!" Ava's voice still rings in my mind. "You're so damned good!"

We were not good for each other. Kismet. Why did I go into that bar? Why did I meet you? Why did you decide to take me home to your web? I asked you one time, "Why me?" You answered, "You had perfect teeth." The answer stunned me. Perfect teeth? There was no logic to it at all.

And all the time I thought it was my charm, my sense of humor, my physical build. It was my teeth? I felt like a horse that had passed a test. The next test – was I a gelding or a stallion?

Rummaging through my mind, I think I should move to another neighborhood, not go to the bars in the old hangouts. Chicago is a good place to blend in, hide out. Change my name and try to get a different kind of job, any job. One that doesn't need a left hand. You had stabbed and put a knife blade through my left hand.

So I wander around, find a cheap room – very cheap, eight bucks a week, no overnight guests. It consists of a single bed, a straight tan chair covered with scarred paint, a metal standing container for my clothes, a stained maple dresser (couple of cigarette burns on it). That is it. What do you expect for eight bucks? Payable every Friday night by 8:00 p.m. or else you are locked out.

I arrange my meager belongings and prepare to march forth into nothing.

Forward, ever forward. I thought the words sounded stilted and corny. Now I am expected to meet some kind of challenge, to march out into nothing, unable to see the shape of the foe; the words sound even more ridiculous.

Here I am with a useless left hand, wounded physically, emotionally. Mentally trying to heal, my mind says, "I love you." Am I mad? You're damned right. I'm an artist. I create. I don't destroy.

In this wonderful eight-dollar room, I fall asleep; I am sleeping in an unguarded place. Strange noises come from people I don't know tramping down the hall to the communal bathroom. Some drunk had fallen asleep after going into the toilet, sitting down, passing out into an alcoholic stupor, locking the bathroom door from the inside, causing chaos.

Frantic pounding wakes me up, banging on the bathroom door by other roomers who have urgent needs.

I don't know where I am, all this noise. My heart races in my chest. I have trouble breathing. I am afraid. Then I remember I am in a rented room; this ten-by-ten-foot box is my new world. I am safe if I stay inside it. I think.

Someone down the hall is pounding on a door. It is all very strange.

It is around Christmastime. Some bizarre Noel night this is. In this building is insanity; outside, soft white snowflakes settle down to cover the dirt of the city. Welcome to the world, baby Jesus, you poor baby.

CHAPTER 16

Years later, upon review, I recall and think the words of the Irish writer Oscar Wilde: "A brave man kills with a sword, a coward with a kiss." Maybe these words applied to us. Your steak knife was your sword, and you felt threatened by my loving you. Had no one ever loved you before? Was your outer beauty a curse for you? Did you feel like a discarded piece of meat – unnecessary, in need but unneeded?

If only I had had more insight, compassion, I might have been able to help you, but ours was a blazing physical lust – the language of sex; it was the only language you knew. You had been taught well by others since you were dumped out on the street at eleven years old.

I understand much more now. I didn't stop loving you. I just ran out of blood. I can't change all those hurtful things in your life nor in my life. I am only human. I feel exhausted, numb. It is time for me to get in my canoe, go to the middle of the lake; I'll be staying there for a lifetime or two.

What the hell, in twenty or thirty years, I'll get over you.